This edition published by Parragon Books Ltd in 2016 and distributed by

Parragon Inc.
440 Park Avenue South, 13th Floor
New York, NY 10016
www.parragon.com

Copyright © Parragon Books Ltd 2016

Retold by Rachel Elliot   Illustrated by Xuân Thanh Lê
Edited by Grace Harvey   Designed by Karissa Santos and Duck Egg Blue
Production by Danielle Nevin

ISBN 978-1-4748-6042-0

Printed in China

JONAH and the WHALE

PaRragon

Bath • New York • Cologne • Melbourne • Delhi
Hong Kong • Shenzhen • Singapore

Jonah lived a simple life in a small village and kept to himself. He liked to sit in the sun outside his house and feed the birds. He didn't like to get involved in other people's problems.

But, one day, Jonah heard a voice that seemed to come from nowhere.

"Jonah, son of Amittai, you will be my prophet," it said.

Jonah jumped to his feet and looked around, but he could see no one.

Then, the voice spoke again, and Jonah knew that it was the voice of God.

"Go to the city of Nineveh and tell the people that they have been very wicked," God said. "Tell them that, if they don't change their ways, I will destroy the city."

Jonah shook with fear.

"Me?" he thought. "God wants me to leave here and go all the way to Nineveh? Who would listen to an unimportant Israelite like me?"

He didn't care about the Ninevites, their wickedness, or their city, and he thought they deserved to be punished by God. Why would God have chosen him? It must be a mistake. Jonah decided to ignore the voice. But God cannot be ignored.

"Jonah, hurry yourself," He said. "Get yourself to Nineveh!"

Jonah gathered some food and water for the journey, but he felt worried and annoyed. The same thought kept running through his mind: "I don't want to get involved in the Ninevites' problems. I just want to be left alone."

Jonah decided to run away to avoid doing God's work. So he left his home, but he did not set out for Nineveh. Instead, he headed for Joppa, a sea port, and got on a ship that was going to Tarshish.

"Maybe God won't notice that I am traveling in the wrong direction," Jonah thought. "By the time I get to Tarshish, it will be too late. I will be so far away from Nineveh that God will have to find Himself a new prophet!"

The sun beat down on Jonah's face and he started to relax. Perhaps he really could avoid God's plan for him. The ship left Joppa, and Jonah heaved a sigh of relief.

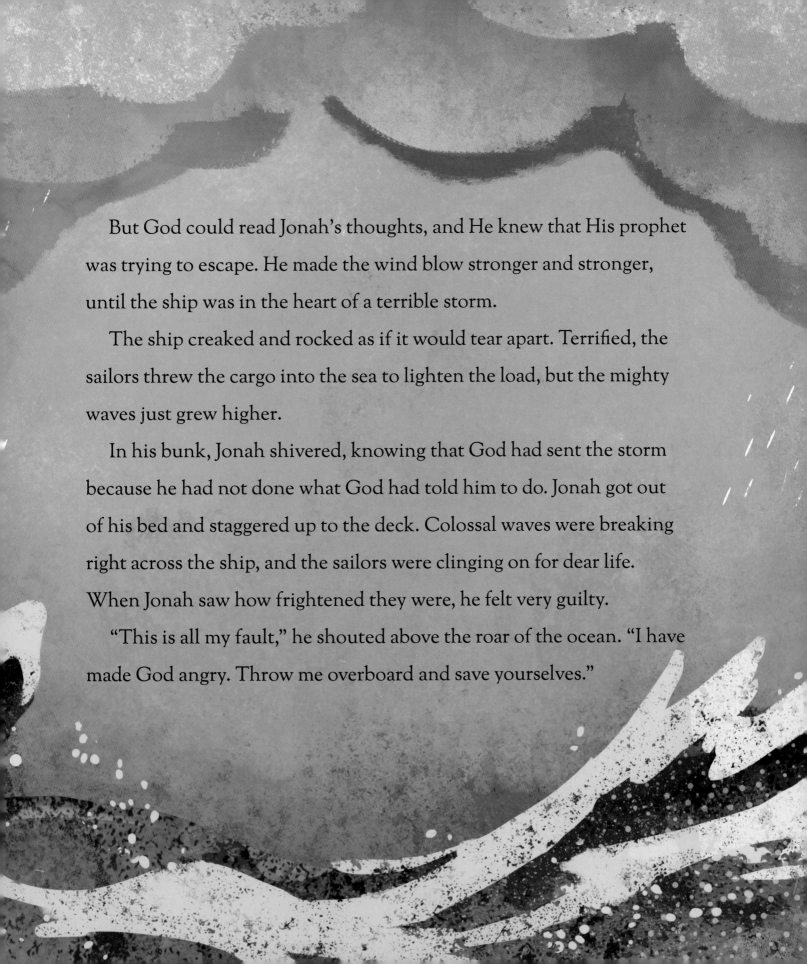

But God could read Jonah's thoughts, and He knew that His prophet was trying to escape. He made the wind blow stronger and stronger, until the ship was in the heart of a terrible storm.

The ship creaked and rocked as if it would tear apart. Terrified, the sailors threw the cargo into the sea to lighten the load, but the mighty waves just grew higher.

In his bunk, Jonah shivered, knowing that God had sent the storm because he had not done what God had told him to do. Jonah got out of his bed and staggered up to the deck. Colossal waves were breaking right across the ship, and the sailors were clinging on for dear life. When Jonah saw how frightened they were, he felt very guilty.

"This is all my fault," he shouted above the roar of the ocean. "I have made God angry. Throw me overboard and save yourselves."

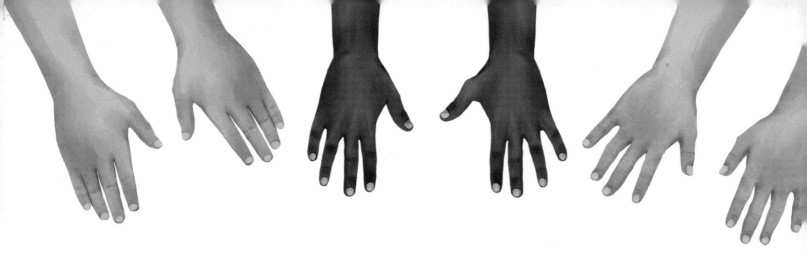

At first, the captain refused to throw his passenger overboard, but the sea became wilder. Hail lashed the decks, and bitter winds tore at the sailors. Desperate to save their lives, the sailors pushed Jonah into the cold sea.

"God, help me, please!" cried Jonah as he fell.

Water closed over Jonah's head, and filled his nose and mouth.
He rose to the surface, coughing and spluttering. Although he was
frightened, he could see that the sea was growing calmer and the wind
dying down. The hail had stopped.

"Thank goodness," said Jonah. "Whatever happens to me, the ship
and all the sailors are safe."

Suddenly, Jonah felt himself being sucked into darkness.

"I'm going to drown!" he thought.

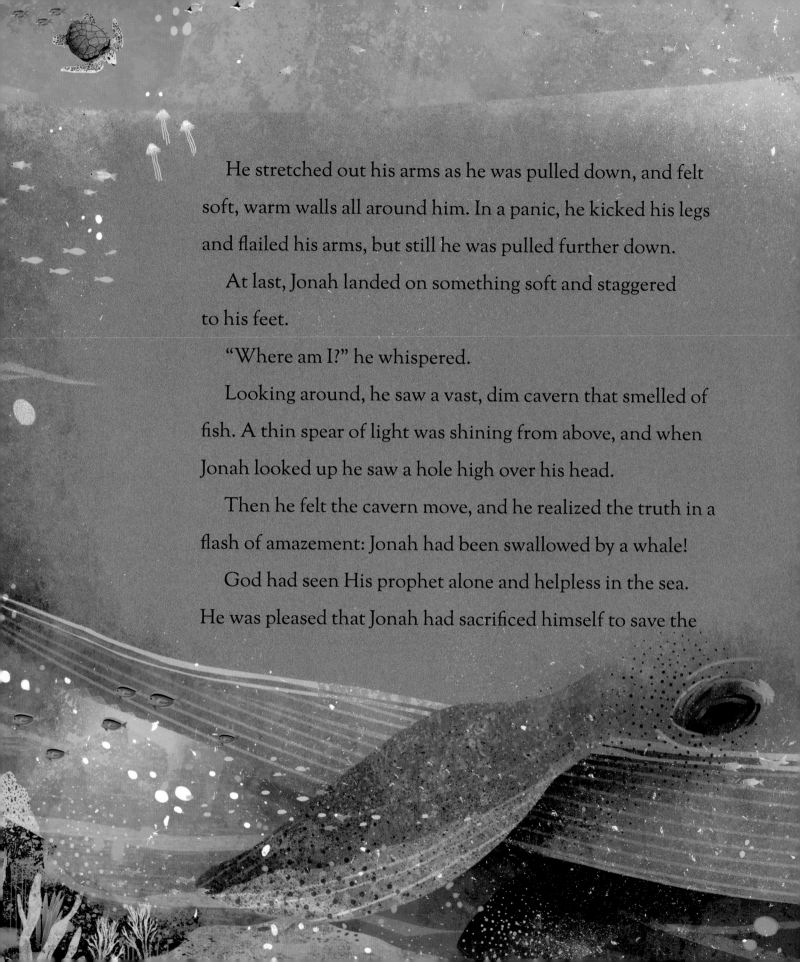

He stretched out his arms as he was pulled down, and felt soft, warm walls all around him. In a panic, he kicked his legs and flailed his arms, but still he was pulled further down.

At last, Jonah landed on something soft and staggered to his feet.

"Where am I?" he whispered.

Looking around, he saw a vast, dim cavern that smelled of fish. A thin spear of light was shining from above, and when Jonah looked up he saw a hole high over his head.

Then he felt the cavern move, and he realized the truth in a flash of amazement: Jonah had been swallowed by a whale!

God had seen His prophet alone and helpless in the sea. He was pleased that Jonah had sacrificed himself to save the

sailors, so He had sent the whale to keep Jonah safe.

Kneeling down, Jonah spoke to God. "I am sorry for disobeying you," he said. "Please let me out of here!"

There was no reply. Jonah beat his hands against the side of the whale, but he could not escape.

Jonah lay inside the whale for three days and three nights. He was tired, wet, and cold, and he felt weak with hunger and thirst. Worst of all, he was gripped by fear. What if he were stuck inside the whale forever? What was God's plan for him?

At last, Jonah shut his eyes and prayed.

"God, I am ready," he whispered into the darkness. "I will gladly do what you asked."

Suddenly, everything started to shake, and light flooded the cavern. Jonah squeezed his eyes shut as he tumbled head over heels through the whale.

"What is happening?" he cried.

When Jonah opened his eyes, he was lying on soft, warm sand. The whale had thrown him up onto dry land. Then Jonah heard God's voice once again.

"Go to the city of Nineveh, Jonah," said God. "Do what I have asked of you."

"I will," Jonah promised.

He climbed to his feet and set off right away.

When he arrived in Nineveh, Jonah thought that no one would believe he was a prophet. But he kept his promise and preached in marketplaces. He spread God's message from slums to palaces, in temples, and in shacks.

"Turn to God and repent, or He will punish you," Jonah told the people.

To his surprise, people stopped to hear him speak. They believed what he said, and God's word spread.

Even the King of Nineveh listened to Jonah's message. He changed his royal robes for clothes made of sackcloth, to show how sad he was.

"No one in Nineveh will eat or drink until we have shown God that we are sorry for all the things we have done wrong," said the king. "I hope that He will be able to forgive us."

God heard Nineveh's prayers and was pleased with Jonah.

"I will not destroy the city," He told Jonah. "They have obeyed me, so I will show mercy."

But, instead of feeling proud for having helped save the city, Jonah felt anger raging inside him. Why hadn't the Ninevites been punished?

"The Ninevites don't deserve to be forgiven!" he cried.

"Is it right for you to be angry?" asked God.

Jonah did not reply. He stormed out of the city—but soon the scorching midday sun was burning down on his head.

Jonah staggered to the side of the road
and dropped to the ground under a bare tree.
He was exhausted and furious, and there
was no shelter from the sun.

"I wish I had never come here," he fumed.
"I didn't ask to get involved."

As Jonah sat there in a rage, God made fresh, green leaves unfurl from the bare branches of the tree. The tree grew larger and curved itself over Jonah, until he was lying in its shade. As his body cooled down, his temper cooled, too.

"Thank you, God," he murmured as he drifted off to sleep.

At sunrise, God sent a worm to eat Jonah's tree. Its leaves shriveled up and fell from the branches. Jonah awoke to find the sun blazing down on him again.

"Why did you kill the tree, God?" Jonah raged. "It was a good tree and provided me with shelter."

"You are angry because the tree did not deserve to die," God said. "How would I have felt if I'd had to let Nineveh burn? If the tree deserves a second chance, surely my people deserve a second chance, too? And what about you, and the whale who saved you?"

Jonah bowed his head in shame. Now, he could see what God was trying to show him.

"I'm sorry," he whispered.

God had saved the people of Nineveh, just as He had sent the whale to save Jonah, because God loves all His people.

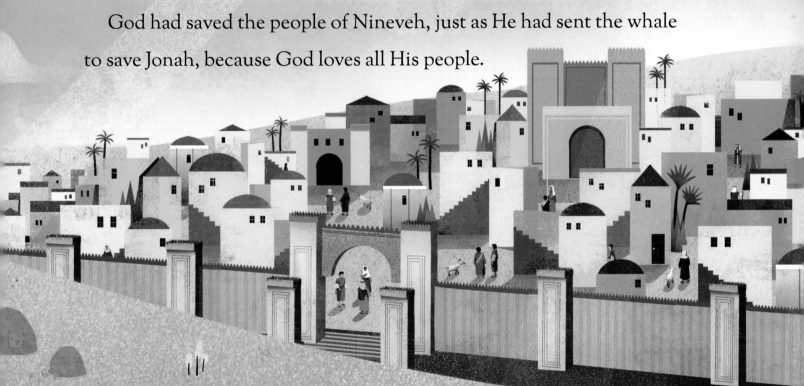